DISNEP

FROZEN
A COOL CONTEST

Written by
ELLE D. RISCO

Illustrated by the
DISNEY STORYBOOK ART TEAM

DISNEP PRESS

Los Angeles • New York

Printed in China
First Box Set Edition, August 2016
3 5 7 9 10 8 6 4 2
FAC-025393-16185
ISBN 978-1-4847-7384-0

Today is the big
ice-carving contest.
Elsa is the judge.

Anna and Olaf
are a team.
They find their ice.

Anna and Olaf have never
carved ice before.
They think it will be fun.

Kristoff and Sven
are a team.
They find their ice.

Kristoff and Sven know
all about ice.
Ice is their life.

Kristoff looks at Anna.
He did not know
she was in the contest.

Anna looks at Kristoff.
She did not know
he was in the contest.

Elsa explains the rules.
Each team has until
the end of the day.
The best carving will win.

"Good luck," Anna says.
"May the best artist win!"
Kristoff says.

Anna and Olaf
start their carving.
They chip away
at their ice!

Kristoff and Sven
take their time.
They search the ice
for lines and cracks.

Kristoff puts his ear
to the ice.
He listens to the ice.

Anna looks at Kristoff.
What is he doing?
Ice does not talk!

Anna and Olaf put
down their tools.
Anna looks at her ice.
She listens to her ice.

Anna sees the cracks
in the ice.
Now she knows where
it will break.

Anna and Olaf get
back to work.
They happily chip away
at their ice.

Kristoff looks at
Anna and Olaf.
They are having fun.
Their ice is taking shape.

Kristoff looks at his ice.
It does not look like anything.
Maybe he and Sven
need to have more fun!

Kristoff whispers to Sven.
He has an idea.

Kristoff and Sven
get back to work.
They work faster.
They are having fun, too.

Hours tick by.
Kristoff and Sven
work on their ice.

Anna and Olaf
work on their ice.
The other teams
work on their ice, too.

The sun sets.
The contest is over.
It is time for Elsa
to pick the winner.

Elsa looks at
each team's carving.
The other teams
have all finished.

Elsa looks at
Kristoff and Sven's ice.
It looks nice, but
it is not done.

Elsa looks at
Anna and Olaf's ice.
It is done, but Elsa
cannot tell what they carved.

"Gerda and Kai
are the winners!"
Elsa says.

Anna and Kristoff clap
for their friends.
"Better luck next time,"
Elsa tells Anna and Kristoff.

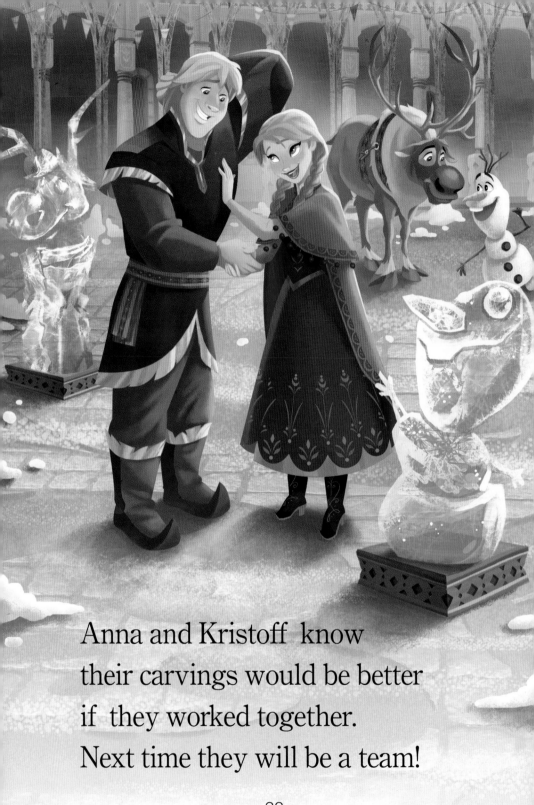

Anna and Kristoff know
their carvings would be better
if they worked together.
Next time they will be a team!